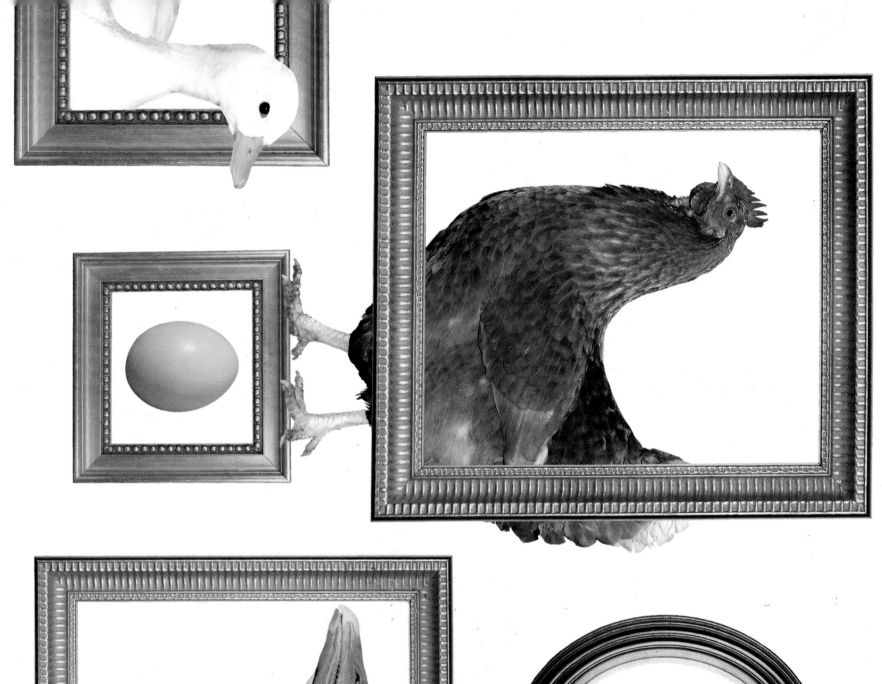

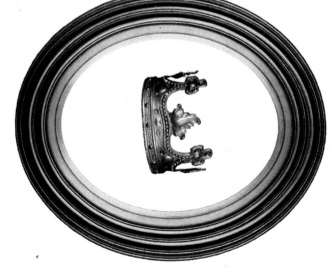

HENNY-PENNY

retold and illustrated by

JANE WATTENBERG

Scholastic Press
NEW YORK

NEXT
8 MILES

STORMY SKIES and whirling winds

flip-flapped around the barnyard. Henny-Penny scratched about for a tasty bite to eat,

when...

WHACK!

An acorn SMACKED Henny-Penny right on top of her fine red comb.

"CHICKABUNGA!" squawked Henny-Penny in alarm.

"THE SKY IS FALLING! IT'S COMING ON DOWN! I must *RUN* and tell the King."

So she **RAN** and **RAN**. That she-hen, she **HUSTLED**, she **HURRIED**, and she **BUMPED** right into that he-chicken, Cocky-Locky, a rooster of fine repute.

Mrs. Mustard's **WORLD MAP**

"What's clickin', chicken?"
pauwk, pauwked Cocky-Locky.

"SHAKE, RATTLE, AND ROLL!
THE SKY IS FALLING!
IT'S COMING ON DOWN!
I'm *LICKETY-SPLIT* to tell the King."

"Well, Hen-Pen, may I flap feathers
and fly with you?"

"DEAR DUMPLING, OH DO!
LET'S *ROCKET*, ROOSTER!"

And away they *RACED* to tell that King.

They **ZIGGED** and **ZAGGED** and **SPED** along

when they met up with one Ducky-Lucky

and one Drake-Cake.

"What's buzzin', cousins?"

breezed Ducky-Lucky and Drake-Cake.

"SHAKE, RATTLE, AND ROLL!

THE SKY IS FALLING!

IT'S COMING ON DOWN!

Henny-Penny saw it and heard it

and it SMACKED her on her fine red comb.

We're *ON THE MOVE* to tell the King,"

crowed Cocky-Locky.

OASIS →

"CREAKY BEAKS!

May we flap along, too?" quacked you-know-who.

"Sure. *SHAKE A WING! LET'S DART, DUCKS!*"

And away they *RACED* to tell that King.

They *BUZZED* down the road straight into that GLAM-GAL Goosey-Loosey and that HE-HUNK, Gander-Lander.

"What words, birds? Why so flighty?" squonked Goosey-Loosey and Gander-Lander.

"SHAKE, RATTLE, AND ROLL!
THE SKY IS FALLING!
IT'S COMING ON DOWN! Henny-Penny saw it and heard it and it SMACKED her on her fine red comb. We're *FULL TILT* to tell the King," raved Ducky-Lucky and Drake-Cake.

"GREAT GOSLINGS!
LET'S JUMP, GOOSE-BUMP!"
honked Gander-Lander.
And away they RACED to tell that King.

FROG
CAMPGROUND
JCT 1/4 MILE

By and by, while on the fly, they *BLEW* into Turkey-Lurkey.

"Why the SCOWL, fowl?" gobbled Turkey-Lurkey.

"SHAKE, RATTLE, AND ROLL!
THE SKY IS FALLING!

IT'S COMING ON DOWN! Henny-Penny saw it and heard it and it SMACKED her on her fine red comb. We're *ZIPPIN'* to tell the King," thundered Gander-Lander.

"**BROODY!**" snapped Turkey-Lurkey.

"May I flock along?"

"Sure, but don't loiter, Lurkey. LET'S *LAUNCH!*
FULL THROTTLE! And away they *RACED*

to tell that King.

Pell-mell and after a spell, they *COLLIDED*
with that **MEAN** ball of fur,
Foxy-Loxy.

"*Going bonkers, bonkers?*

Out in such **FOWL** weather?" Foxy-Loxy asked

Henny-Penny, Cocky-Locky, Ducky-Lucky, Drake-Cake,

Goosey-Loosey, Gander-Lander, and Turkey-Lurkey.

"SHAKE, RATTLE, AND ROLL!
THE SKY IS FALLING!
IT'S COMING ON DOWN! Henny-Penny saw it

and heard it and it SMACKED her on her fine red comb.

We're *STEAMIN'* to tell the King," rattled Turkey-Lurkey.

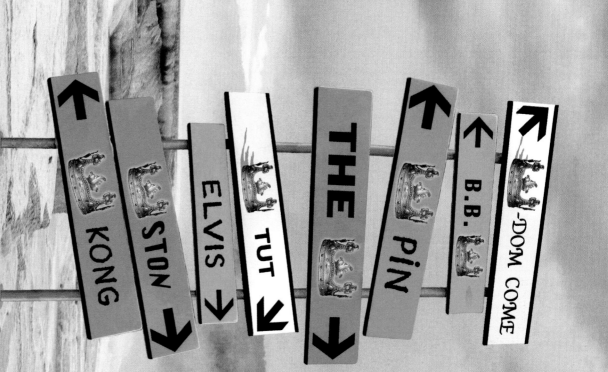

"*Ooh murky, turkey,*" drooled Foxy-Loxy. But he smiled as though it might not be as BEASTLY BAD as all that.

"Do you fine feathered friends know the FAST TRACK to the King?"

KONG

STON

ELVIS

TUT

THE

PIN

B.B.

"-DOM COME

Turkey-Lurkey looked at Gander-Lander,

Gander-Lander looked at Goosey-Loosey,

Goosey-Loosey looked at Drake-Cake,

Drake-Cake looked at Ducky-Lucky,

Ducky-Lucky looked at Cocky-Locky,

Cocky-Locky looked at Henny-Penny,

who shook her red head

NO!

Throw in the towel, Fowl, thought Foxy-Loxy as he considered the FINE DINNER coming his way.

But with IMPECCABLE MANNERS and CHARMING HOSPITALITY, he *REALLY* said,

"You're in LUCK, Duck.

Looking JUICY, Goosey.

If I knew you were coming
I'd have BAKED A CAKE, Drake.

"Turkey-JERKY, Lurkey?

Let's MEANDER, Gander.

Lead the FLOCK, Lock.

And so we meet again, HEN.

It will be my **PLEASURE** to show you the way."

Foxy-Loxy led them toward a **dank, dark, dark cave** by the side of a **dark, dank riverbank.** Turkey-Lurkey was the first one in.

GRIZZLY BEAR AREA
SPECIAL RULES APPLY.

FOXY-LOXY'S LUNCH ROOM

LEAPING GIZZARDS!
WHAT A SKANKY PRANK!

For with a GOBBLE-GOBBLE-GOBBLE!

that sly Foxy-Loxy *wolfed down*

poor Turkey-Lurkey.

With a SQUONK-HISS-S-S-S-HONK!

that fleazy Foxy-Loxy *gobbled up*

Goosey-Loosey and Gander-Lander.

With a QUACK! DON'T LOOK BACK!

that cunning cad Foxy-Loxy *wolfed down*

Ducky-Lucky and Drake-Cake.

With a COCK-A-DOODLE-DOO! WHAT
DID I DO TO YOU? that greedy grunge

of a Foxy-Loxy *gobbled up*

poor Cocky-Locky.

TAKE OUT

But when Henny-Penny heard Cocky-Locky crow, she cluck, cluck, clucked, "**CHICKA-CHICKA-BUNGA! I FORGOT** TO LAY MY **EGG** TODAY!"

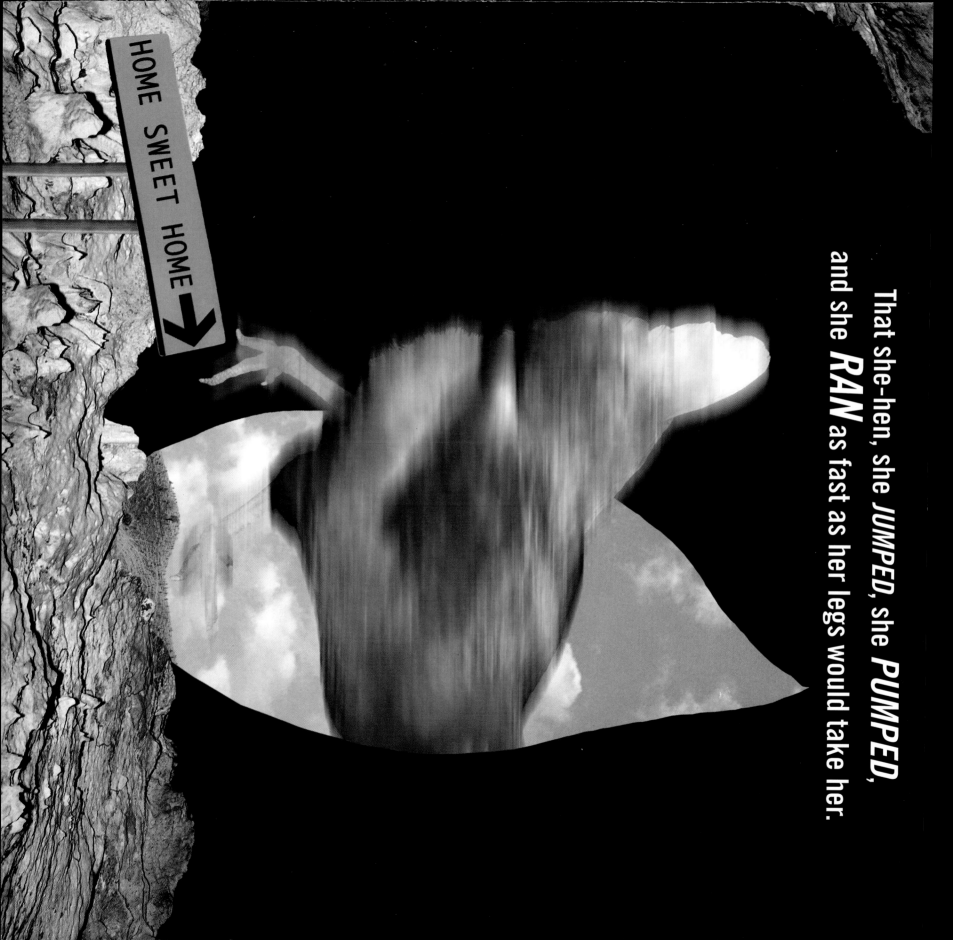

That she-hen, she *JUMPED*, she *PUMPED*, and she *RAN* as fast as her legs would take her.

HOME SWEET HOME →

She never **DID** tell the King ---------- the sky was falling.

STOP
HERE FOR
HEN

LUCKY PLUCKY EGGS

For Seymour & Ruth Wattenberg,
who always kept the sky from falling.

L I B R A R Y   O F   C O N G R E S S   C A T A L O G I N G - I N - P U B L I C A T I O N   D A T A

Wattenberg, Jane. Henny-Penny / retold and illustrated by Jane Wattenberg. —1st ed.   p. cm.   SUMMARY: While

on their way to tell the king that the sky is falling, Henny-Penny and her friends meet the very hungry Foxy-Loxy.

[1. Folklore.] I. Chicken-Licken. II. Title.   PZ8.1.W37 H1 2000   398.24'528625—dc21   [E]   99-28806   CIP

ISBN: 0-439-07817-2

Printed in Mexico   49   First edition, April 2000

10 9 8 7 6 5 4 3   0/0 1 2 3 4

The illustrations in this book were created in Adobe Photoshop using photographs of the author's own

friendly fowls. The text type was set in Trade Gothic Bold Condensed. The display type was set in

Freestyle Script. Book design by Jane Wattenberg and David Saylor

And **ULTRA THANKS** to: Andy and Kristen Sulonen and their chickens! Kraut Pheasant

Farms and their turkeys! Walt Leonard and his geese! Irma and Harold Schwartz for

their contagious farming spirit. Tracy Mack and David Saylor, heaven-sent,

best of the best! Kendra Marcus—what ideas! clarity! and forward

ho! My lovely Henny-Penny, Beata, whose sky did fall. My

sons, Isaiah, Solomon, and Gideon, my terra firma.

Samuel, my big blue sky, forever.

THE END

WHAT'S FAIR IS FOWL,
WHAT'S FOWL IS FARE.

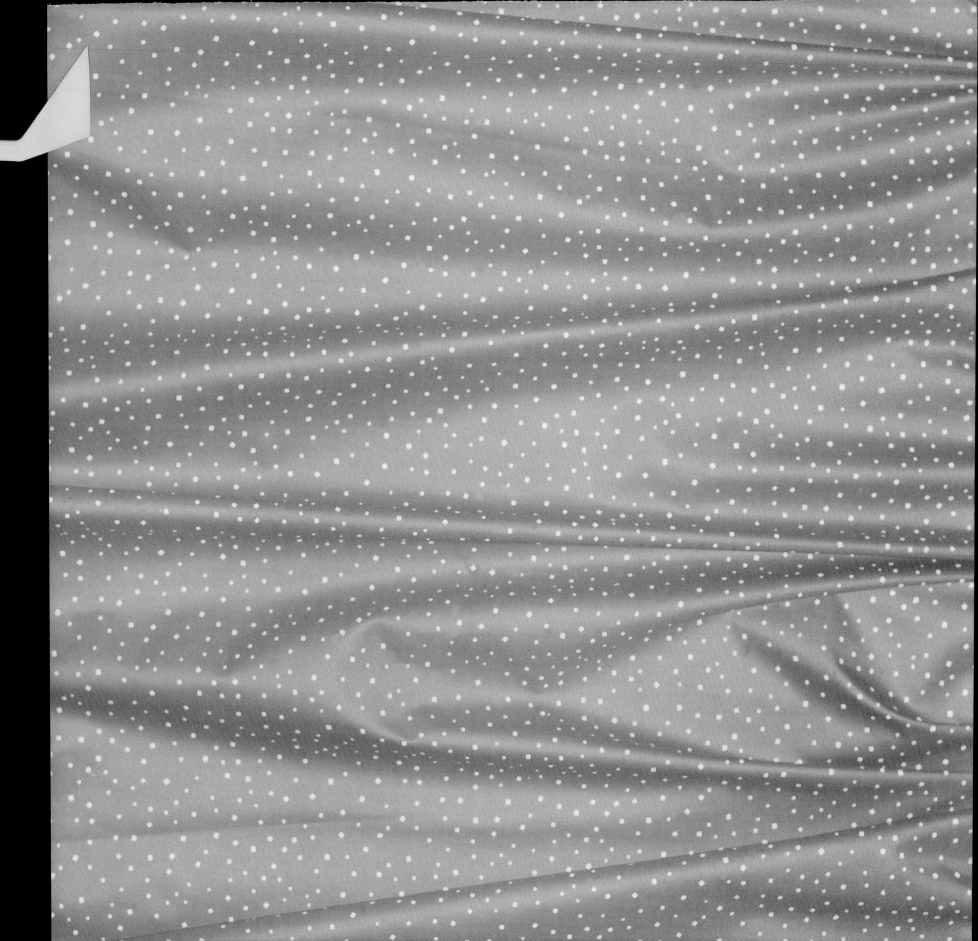

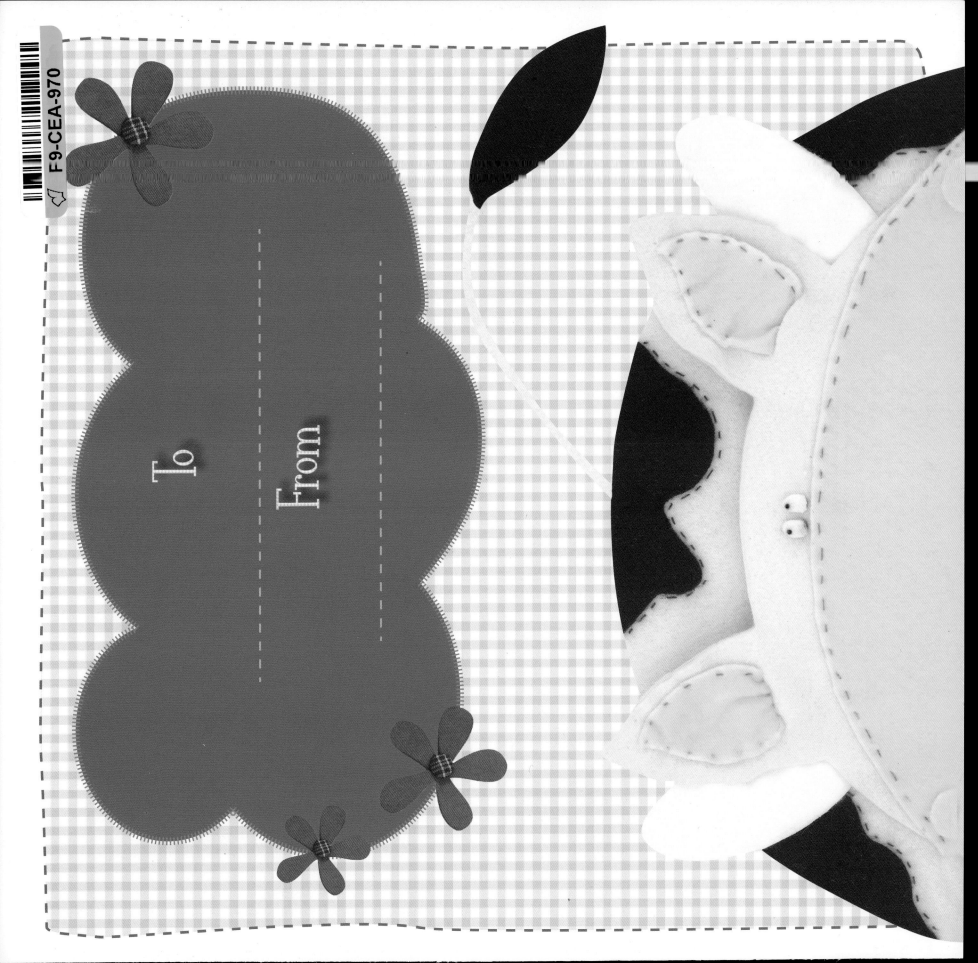

To

From

Inspired by Holly Reagan
With thanks to Jane Horne
and Claire Page

This edition first published in 2010 by Castle Street Press
an imprint of make believe ideas ltd

Copyright © 2007
make believe ideas ltd.

27 Castle Street, Berkhamsted,
Hertfordshire, HP4 2DW.
565, Royal Parkway, Nashville, TN 37214, USA.

Manufactured in China

squ-e-e-eze!

I love

I love everything about you:

Your tail, your ears, your toes.

I love the softness of your skin.

your silky, s-moo-th, wet nose.

I love your every moo-vement.

the way you skip about.

point inwards,

hooves

and how your

point inwards.

while all your **knees** stick out!

I love the way
you chatter,
the funny things you say,
the **moo**–sic
that you sing to me,

the silly games we play.

And when you
go exploring,

tweet! tweet! tweet!

DoG

Grrr!

It makes me really proud.

to know you'll always find me.

moo! moo! moo! moo! moo! moo! moo!

even in a crowd.

At nighttime, in the moo-nlight, when the stars shine overhead.

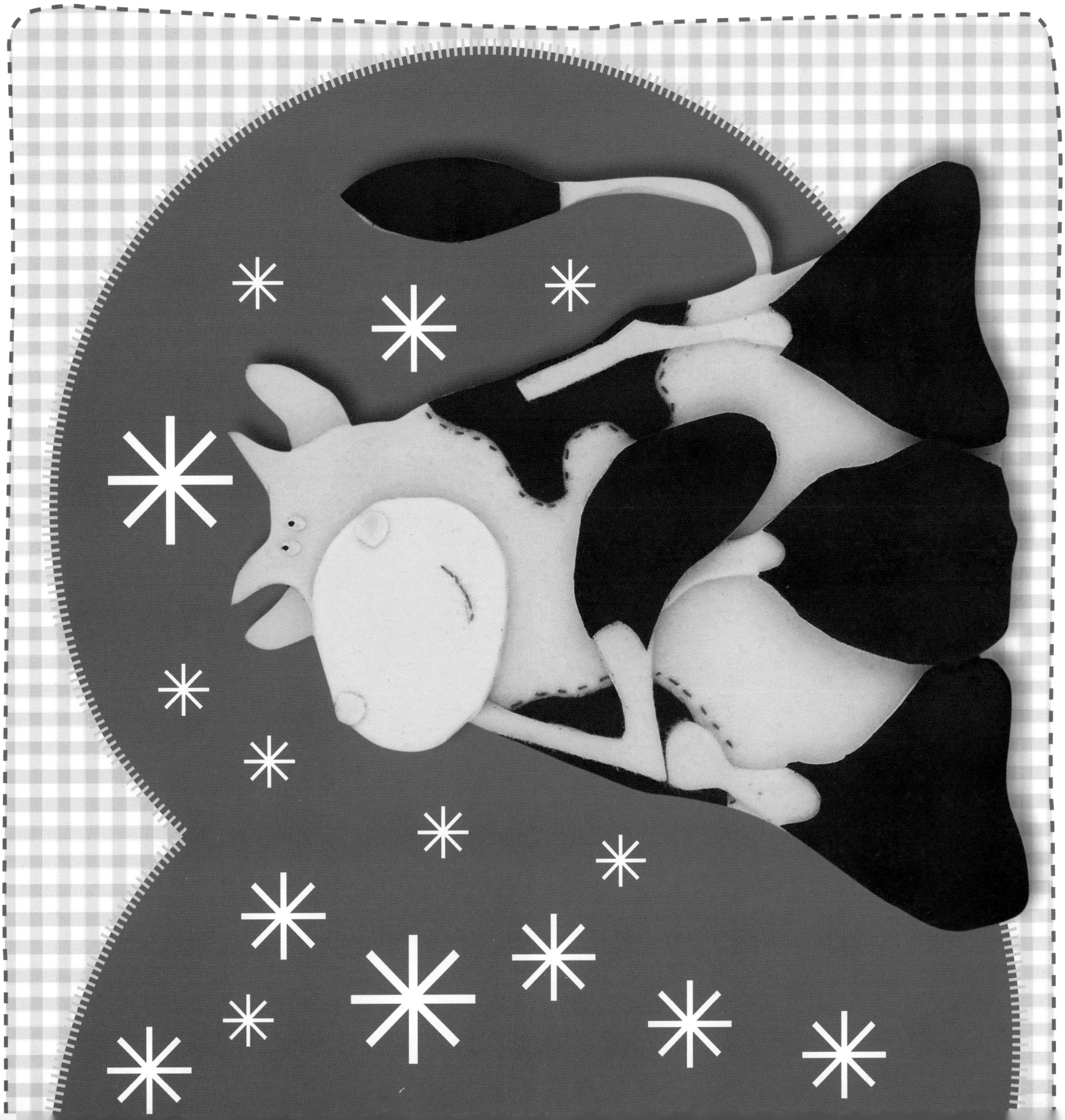

I watch you as you're sleeping in your snuggly, little bed.

Even when you're not meaning to be bad.

moo-dy,

Every day with you is special,

through and through,

I love you

I love you

I UDDERLY, UDDERLY LOVE YOU

and I know you love me too!

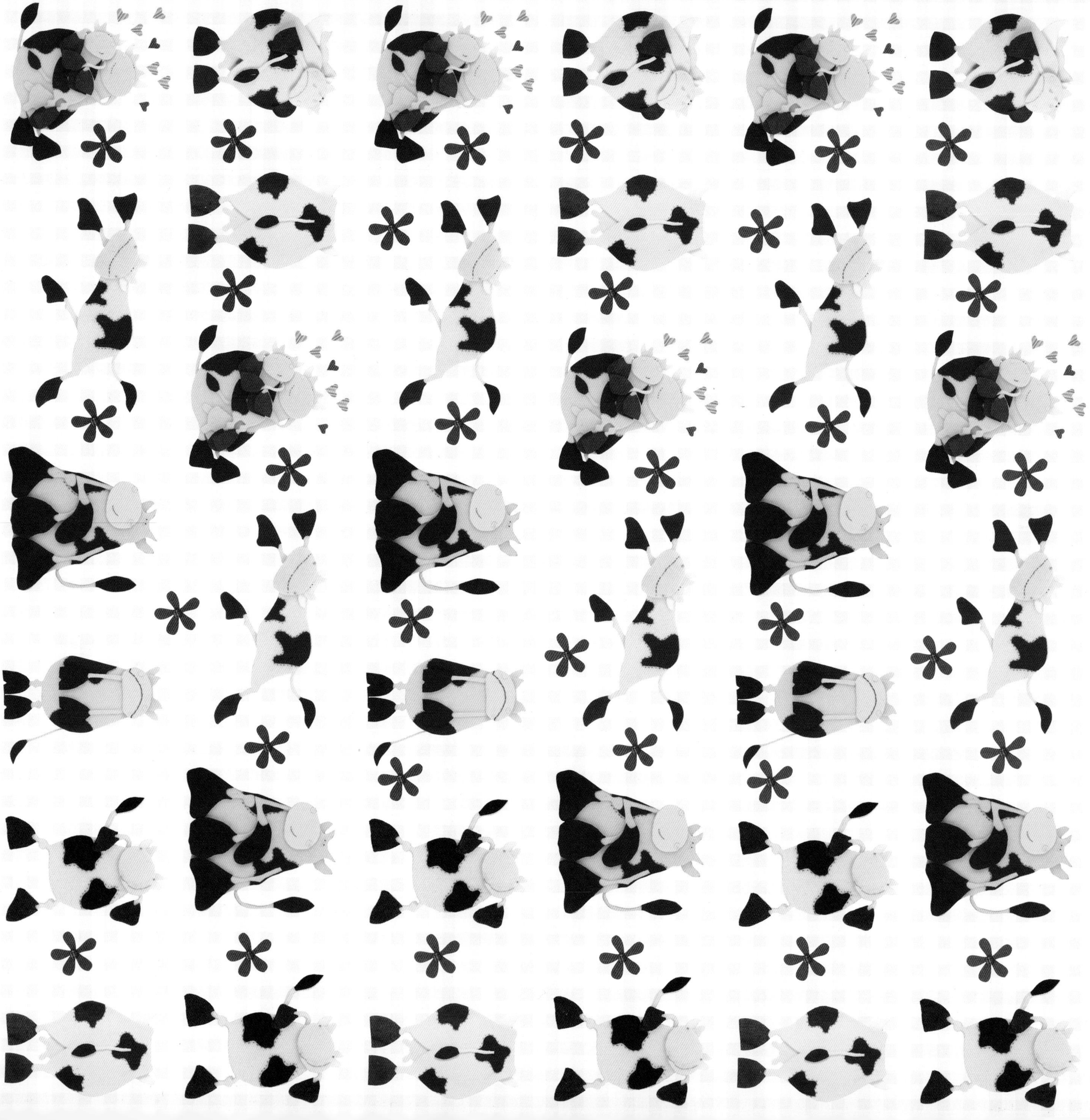